Coco-Chan's KIMONO

Kumiko Sudo

Breckling Press

Library of Congress Cataloging-in-Publication Data

Cataloging data is available from the Library of Congress.

This book was set in By George Titling

Editorial and art direction by Anne Knudsen

Design and production by Maria Mann

Special thanks to Joanna Spathis for her help with the text

Published by Breckling Press

283 N. Michigan St, Elmhurst, IL 60126

Developed and produced in the United States

Printed and bound in China.

International Standard Book Number (ISBN 13): 978-1-933308-26-5

Dedication

In memory of my aunt, who sewed many kimonos for me
when I was her little Coco-Chan.

As Mama sews, Coco-chan peeks at her new kimono.
Blues and yellows, pinks and golds, she can't wait to try it on.
"Why don't you make-believe a tea party," suggests Mama,
"or make a paper crane? Remember, fold a thousand
cranes and your wishes will be heard."

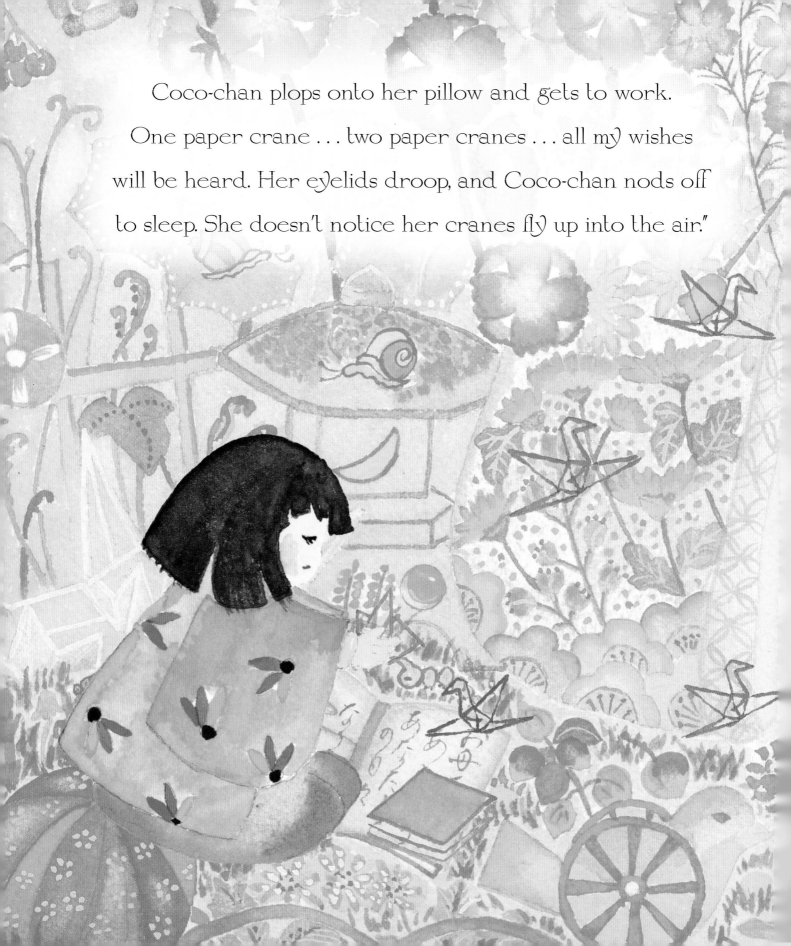

Coco-chan plops onto her pillow and gets to work.
One paper crane . . . two paper cranes . . . all my wishes
will be heard. Her eyelids droop, and Coco-chan nods off
to sleep. She doesn't notice her cranes fly up into the air."

A lazy breeze drifts by, with a dragonfly
in its trail. "Achoo! Achoo," he blows, "Such breezes
bring sneezes!" Coco-chan wakes with a start.
Mr. Dragonfly winks, inviting her to come with him.

Coco-chan slips off the veranda and steps into
a world of creatures large and small.

"Wait for me," she cries, while her new friend flits into a tangle of dandelions. Coco-chan follows. "Where did he go?" she wonders, as she crawls out the other side and finds that she's alone.

But wait! Who's there? A ladybug steps forward to greet her, bowing sweetly. "I don't wish to be rude," the ladybug says, "but is there something to eat? The cranes invited me to tea, you see."

Coco-chan brews the tea and a courteous caterpillar
helps her serve. Songbirds entertain the waiting guests.
Coco-chan hopes there is enough tea to go around.

After tea, Coco-chan says goodbye to her new friends
and decides it's time to explore.

The garden grows tall around her, so Coco-chan finds two twigs that are just the right size. She totters on through sunshine and shadow . . . with a better view.

Before long, Coco-chan meets a pair of caterpillars and stops to chat. They will soon learn to fly, they say. Coco-chan wonders if she might try it, too.

The sky brightens, and two butterflies dance into the air.
Knowing that anything is possible, Coco-chan holds
out her arms and lets the wind lift her. Up she goes!
The garden stretches below, like a kimono
sprinkled with the flowers of Spring.

After all the excitement, Coco-chan needs a moment of calm.

A slither in the grass pulls her out of her meditation.

A snake coils up neatly below her. "Sh- sh- should you wish,

you may stroll along with me," he says.

He leads Coco-chan to a grassy bank, where all her garden friends are gathered. She tells them of her adventures.

The sunlight fades and Coco-chan knows it's time to go home.

A shy chick scuttles forward with an invitation

to return any time she pleases. "But how do I get back?"

Coco-chan asks, "Which way do I go?

Follow me," says the snail, "If you don't mind that I'm slow."

"Our garden is always here, if you have eyes to see.

Beneath every leaf, beside every brook, there are friends

everywhere, once you know how to look."

"Mama is waiting," Coco-chan says with a sigh.

"Don't worry, dear friends, for this isn't goodbye."

"Let us help you get home. Close your eyes and you're there, carried by dreams on wings of fresh air."

With a rustle of leaves and a shimmer of silk, Coco-chan turns to find Mama holding a new kimono.

Coco-chan slips inside the colorful cloth, wrapping herself in a garden of flowers and friendship.

Make a Paper Kimono!

1 Cut a piece of pretty paper or gift wrap to 5" x 15½".

2 Place the paper patterned side down. Draw a line across the paper 2½" from the top. Fold along this line (so that the patterned side shows). Glue in place. You should now see 2½" of pattern. With a sharp pair of scissors, trim off the sharp corners at the top edge of the glued section, creating rounded corners. Make a 1½" slit immediately below the pattern area, right and left.

3 Fold in both sides of the unpatterned section by ½", so that ½" of pattern shows. Fold in the bottom edge by ³⁄₈". Repeat the bottom fold, creating a double fold along the bottom edge.

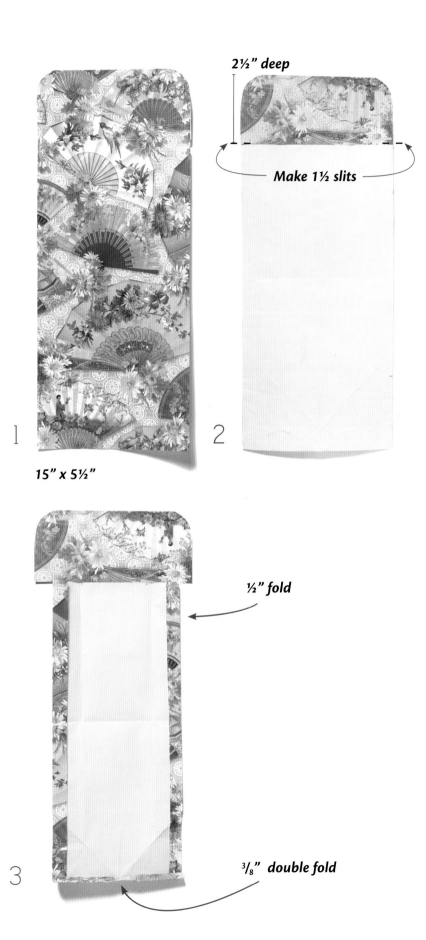

1

15" x 5½"

2½" deep

Make 1½ slits

2

½" fold

3

³⁄₈" double fold

4

4 Flip over the paper, pattern-side up. Find the mid-point of the bottom edge. Starting $\frac{1}{16}$" from the middle point, fold the bottom right corner of the paper upwards, creating a triangle fold. Repeat with the bottom left corner. After making both folds, you should see a vertical gap of $\frac{1}{8}$" between the two parallel edges of the triangle-folded corners.

5 Flip the paper pattern-side down. Measuring from the "point" of the arrow, fold the "point" up $5\frac{1}{8}$" from the tip. The "point" should overlap the bottom edge of the glued section by $\frac{1}{2}$".

$\frac{1}{8}$" **gap**

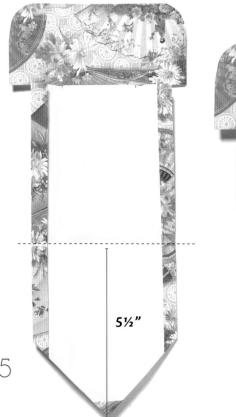

5

5½"

6 Fold the left edge of the paper inward vertically 1" from the left side (at the point where the slit ends). Repeat with the right side.

7 Insert the left edge under the flaps along the vertical edge of the left triangle fold. Repeat with the right side.

8 Fold the top glued part backward along the line created by the two slits. The tip of the "point" should stick up 1/2" above the fold. Your kimono is now complete!

6

1" fold

7

8